BEGINNING HISTORY

PLAGUE AND FIRE

Rhoda Nottridge

Illustrated by Bernard Long

BEGINNING HISTORY

The Age of Exploration
The American West
Crusaders
Egyptian Farmers
Egyptian Pyramids
Family Life in World War II
Greek Cities
The Gunpowder Plot
Medieval Markets
Norman Castles

Plague and Fire
Roman Cities
Roman Soldiers
Saxon Villages
Tudor Sailors
Tudor Towns
Victorian Children
Victorian Factory Workers
Viking Explorers
Viking Warriors

All words that appear in **bold** are explained in the glossary on page 22.

Series Editor: Deborah Elliott
Designer: Helen White

First published in 1990 by Wayland (Publishers) Limited, 61 Western Road,
Hove, East Sussex BN3 1JD

2nd impression 1991

British Library Cataloguing in Publication Data
Nottridge, Rhoda
Plague and fire.
1. London, 1660–1685
I. Title   II. Series
942.1066

ISBN 0–7502–0048–0

Typeset by Kalligraphics Limited, Horley, Surrey.
Printed in Italy by G. Canale & C.S.p.A., Turin.
Bound in Belgium by Casterman, S.A.

CONTENTS

THE CROWDED CITY

London is the huge **capital** city of England. Many years ago, the city was much smaller. Many houses and streets, which are a part of London today, were still fields in those days.

In 1665, over 300 years ago, many people lived in the centre of London. Because it was not as big as it is today, they lived crowded close together in small, wooden houses in narrow, dirty streets.

THE PLAGUE BEGINS

In those days, there were many poor people living in London. Some hardly had enough to eat. But one creature never starved — the rat.

Rats can give **diseases** to humans. People did not know this then. Rats passed on a terrible illness to humans which was called the **plague**. People who caught the illness died within days. The plague spread quickly through the crowded city.

Opposite *This illustration is of a typical London street in the 1600s. Notice how dirty and run-down it looks.*

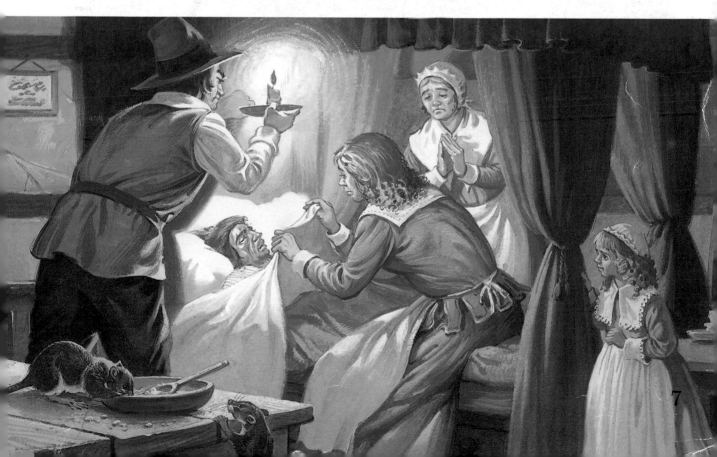

FEAR ON THE STREETS!

Plague victims being lowered into a pit.

Everyone became terrified of catching the plague. They painted red crosses on the doors of houses where someone had the plague, and would not let anyone leave.

This did not stop the plague from spreading, however. Every week thousands of people died. Some people thought God had brought the plague to punish wicked people. But both good and bad people died of the dreadful disease.

Right *An illustration of a scene in London during the terrible days of the plague.*

BRING OUT YOUR DEAD

At night, men with carts cried 'bring out your dead'. They took the dead and threw them into huge **pits**.

Rich people left London to try to escape the plague. Others bought charms bearing the magic word 'abracadabra', hoping they would escape death. Dogs and cats were killed in case they **carried** the plague. But no one killed the rats.

11

THE FINAL COUNT

Over 100,000 people in London died of the plague. It spread across the country, killing thousands more.

When winter came, the plague began to disappear. People returned from the country and opened up their shops and businesses again.

Londoners were glad to be alive. They could not possibly imagine a year more terrible than 1665. Yet worse was to come!

A BAKERY BURNS DOWN

A year after the plague, London had a long, hot summer. The wooden buildings were as dry as firewood. It would only take a few sparks of fire to set a house **alight**.

Those sparks began in a bakery in Pudding Lane. The baker and his family and servants were asleep upstairs. In the bakery below, the dry wood kept to stoke the ovens caught fire. Soon flames spread through the building.

The fire that began in the bakery in Pudding Lane soon spread throughout the city. This painting shows London burning.

FIRE! FIRE!

The baker's family was awoken by neighbours and escaped from the fire by climbing across the roof to the next building.

Everyone tried to put out the fire with buckets of water, but the fire was spreading faster and faster. By dawn, dozens of houses were on fire. A strong wind blew the flames from house to house, across the very narrow streets.

In this picture, you can see the old St. Paul's Cathedral about to catch fire.

TRYING TO ESCAPE

In the streets, people were rushing around. They took whatever **possessions** they could carry from their burning homes. Many crowded on to boats on the River Thames, hoping to escape the flames that were destroying the city. But even the river water boiled with the heat.

Buildings were burnt down and houses were blown up with gunpowder to stop the fire spreading. It **raged** for three days before it could be put out.

A NEW CITY

In the Great Fire over 12,000 houses and many churches were **destroyed**. A huge black cloud of smoke was all that remained.

Plans had to be made. New, wider streets were built, which fires could not leap across.

From that second terrible year in London, a whole new city was built. The Londoners who built it would be very proud to know that many of those new buildings are still standing today.

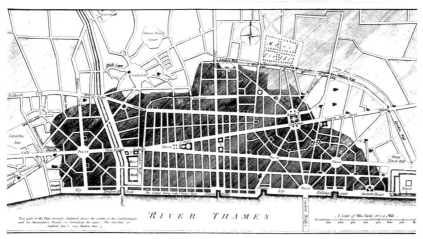

The plan for the new City of London.

Below *The new Covent Garden market.*

GLOSSARY

Alight On fire.

Capital The main city from which a country is ruled.

Carried To carry a disease is to pass an illness one person has on to someone else.

Destroy To completely ruin something, so that there is nothing left.

Diseases Illnesses or sickness that can be passed on from one person to another.

Pits Deep holes which have been dug in the ground.

Plague A disease which is very easy to catch and can affect many people.

Plans Ways of sorting out how to do something in the future.

Possessions Items which belong to someone.

Raged To have been very fierce.

BOOKS TO READ

Stuarts and Georgians by I R Worsnop (Basil Blackwell, 1985)

The Blacksmith's House by Joy James (A & C Black, 1979)

The Fire of London by Rupert Matthews (Wayland, 1988)

INDEX

Picture acknowledgements

The publishers would like to thank the following for providing the photographs in this book: E T Archives Limited 15, 17, 21 (bottom); The Mary Evans Picture Library 6, 8, 9, 21 (top).